Dear Parent:
Your child's love of reading starts here!

Every child learns to read in a different way and at his or her own speed. Some go back and forth between reading levels and read favorite books again and again. Others read through each level in order. You can help your young reader improve and become more confident by encouraging his or her own interests and abilities. From books your child reads with you to the first books he or she reads alone, there are I Can Read Books for every stage of reading:

SHARED READING
Basic language, word repetition, and whimsical illustrations, ideal for sharing with your emergent reader

BEGINNING READING
Short sentences, familiar words, and simple concepts for children eager to read on their own

READING WITH HELP
Engaging stories, longer sentences, and language play for developing readers

3

READING ALONE
Complex plots, challenging vocabulary, and high-interest topics for the independent reader

ADVANCED READING
Short paragraphs, chapters, and exciting themes for the perfect bridge to chapter books

I Can Read Books have introduced children to the joy of reading since 1957. Featuring award-winning authors and illustrators and a fabulous cast of beloved characters, I Can Read Books set the standard for beginning readers.

A lifetime of discovery begins with the magical words **"I Can Read!"**

Visit www.icanread.com for information on enriching your child's reading experience.

For Anne Bezverkov,
who loved books
—H.P.

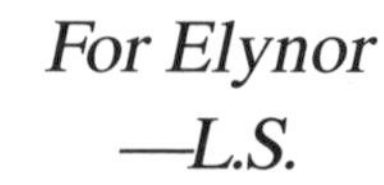

For Elynor
—L.S.

Watercolors and a black pen were used for the full-color art.

HarperCollins®, ®, and I Can Read Book® are trademarks of HarperCollins Publishers.

 For information address HarperCollins Children's Books, a division of HarperCollins Publishers, 10 East 53rd Street, New York, NY 10022. www.harpercollinschildrens.com

---

Library of Congress Cataloging-in-Publication Data

Parish, Herman.
Amelia Bedelia, bookworm / Herman Parish ; pictures by Lynn Sweat.
p. cm.—(An I can read book)
"Greenwillow Books"
Summary: The literal-minded housekeeper causes chaos at her local library when she stops by to help the librarian.
ISBN-10: 0-06-051890-1 (trade bdg.) — ISBN-13: 978-0-06-051890-5 (trade bdg.)
ISBN-10: 0-06-051891-X (lib. bdg.) — ISBN-13: 978-0-06-051891-2 (lib. bdg.)
ISBN-10: 0-06-051892-8 (pbk.) — ISBN-13: 978-0-06-051892-9 (pbk.)
[1. Libraries—Fiction. 2. Humorous stories.] I. Sweat, Lynn, ill. II. Title.
PZ7.P2185 Ao 2003 2002035329
[E]—dc21 CIP
AC

Originally published by Greenwillow Books, an imprint of HarperCollins Publishers in 2003.

14 15 16 17 18 LP/WOR 20 19 18

Amelia Bedelia, Bookworm

story by Herman Parish
pictures by Lynn Sweat

HarperCollins*Publishers*

"Hi, Mrs. Page," said Amelia Bedelia.

"How is the world's best librarian?"

"Amelia Bedelia," said Mrs. Page.

"Am I glad to see you."

“I give up,” said Amelia Bedelia.

“Are you glad to see me?”

“Of course I am,” said Mrs. Page.

“I am just frazzled today.”

“What’s wrong?” said Amelia Bedelia.

“It is my boss,” said Mrs. Page.

“The head librarian is stopping by.

When it comes to libraries and books,

she knows it all.”

"She sounds very smart,"
said Amelia Bedelia.
"Did she invent books?"
"Almost," said Mrs. Page.
"She has been around forever."

“Don’t worry,” said Amelia Bedelia.

“She’ll love your library. The children do.”

“Thank you,” said Mrs. Page.

“I just wish her visit could be special.”

"I will help," said Amelia Bedelia.
"First, I must return some books."
Mrs. Page was astonished.
"What have you done to them?"

“Remember?” said Amelia Bedelia.

“You said these books needed jackets.

So I made a jacket for each one.”

"This book got a sweater,"
said Mrs. Page.
"Sure," said Amelia Bedelia.
"It is about the North Pole.
It gets very cold there."
"Now I have seen everything,"
said Mrs. Page.
"This is one book
you *can* judge by its cover."

"Excuse me," said Mark.

"May I check out this book?"

"Certainly," said Mrs. Page.

"Here is your book, Mark."

"Yippee!" said Amelia Bedelia.

"Free bookmarks for everyone."

"Bookmarks?" said Mrs. Page.

"Who is giving out bookmarks?"

"You are," said a girl.
"You gave that boy a bookmark."
"I did not," said Mrs. Page.
"I said 'Here is your book, *Mark*,'
because that boy is named Mark."

"My name is Danny," said Danny.
"Too bad," said the girl.
"If you were named Mark,
you could have a bookmark."
"That is not fair!" said Danny.

“Amelia Bedelia,” said Mrs. Page,
“see what you have started?”
“I am sorry,” said Amelia Bedelia.

Mrs. Page got paper, scissors, and pens.
"Children, Amelia Bedelia will help each one of you to make a bookmark."
"What about Mark?" said Amelia Bedelia.

"Don't forget him," said Mrs. Page.
"Make him a bookmark, too.
Just be as quiet as you can.
I want to hear a pin drop."

"Okay," said Amelia Bedelia.

She threw her pen on the floor.

"How was that?" said Amelia Bedelia.

"Do you want to hear my pen drop again?"

Mrs. Page shook her head and walked away.

Amelia Bedelia got right to work.
She drew a picture of Mark
on his bookmark.
She made each bookmark special.

“Next!” said Amelia Bedelia.

“What is your name?”

“My name is Ralph,” the next boy said.

“But I don’t need a bookmark.

I need help with my school report.”

“What is it about?” said Amelia Bedelia.

"Dinosaurs," he said. "You know, tyrannosaurus, allosaurus, ste . . . stego . . ."

"Stego Saurus?" said Amelia Bedelia.

"That's the one," said Ralph.

"It figures," said Amelia Bedelia. "If your last name is Saurus, you are probably a dinosaur."

“Excuse me,” said a girl.

“I need some help, too.

I am looking for a thesaurus.”

“The Saurus?” said Amelia Bedelia.

“What kind of dinosaur is that?”

“I’m not sure,” said the girl.

“Is a thesaurus a dinosaur?

My teacher said

I needed one to do my report.”

“Gee,” said Amelia Bedelia,

“you are way too late.

Every Saurus died

millions of years ago.”

“What am I going to do now?”

said the girl.

“Let’s make a bookmark for you,”

said Amelia Bedelia.

“What is your name?”

“My name is Lisa,” she said.
“But I don’t need a bookmark,
because Sam ate my book.”
“Yipes!” said Amelia Bedelia.
“Is Sam okay? Where is he?”
“Sam is fine,” said Lisa.

Lisa pointed out the window.
"Sam is cute," she said,
"but he chews up everything."

"Whew," said Amelia Bedelia.
"I was worried about Sam."
"I am worried, too," said Lisa.
"Mrs. Page will be mad
that her book got wrecked."
"I see," said Amelia Bedelia.
"Let's go talk with her."

“Mrs. Page,” said Amelia Bedelia,

“Lisa has a book checked out.”

Mrs. Page looked up the title.

“Here it is,” said Mrs. Page.

“How to Train Your Dog.”

"That's the book," said Lisa.

"But Sam got it."

Mrs. Page corrected Lisa.

"You mean Sam *has* it.

Did he enjoy it?"

"He sure did," said Amelia Bedelia.

"Sam devoured it."

"Wonderful!" said Mrs. Page.

"We librarians love that."

"You do?" said Amelia Bedelia.

"Oh, yes," said Mrs. Page.

"But it breaks my heart

if a book is abused or lost.

A missing book must be replaced."

"Of course," said Amelia Bedelia.

"Rules are rules," said Mrs. Page.

"You have to go by the book."

"Right," said Amelia Bedelia.

"We have to go buy the book."

"You see," said Mrs. Page,

"lots of people depend on us,

especially those

who cannot visit the library.

I mean, take our bookmobile . . ."

An assistant interrupted her.
"Oh, Mrs. Page, the head librarian will be here in twenty minutes."
"Goodness," said Mrs. Page.
She ran off to get ready.

“Lisa,” said Amelia Bedelia,
“Mrs. Page told us what to do.
We need to go buy the book.
And we can take the bookmobile.”
“May I come, too?” said Lisa.
“Sure,” said Amelia Bedelia.
“Just ask your mother first.”
“Here she comes,” said Lisa.
“She was teaching an art class.”

Lisa's mom gave permission.

"May I ask a favor?"

said Amelia Bedelia.

"These children may need help

with bookmarks and reports."

"I'd be glad to help," Lisa's mom said.

"Thanks," said Amelia Bedelia.

"We'll be right back."

"I love this bookmobile,"
said Lisa.
"Me, too," said Amelia Bedelia.
"Let's pretend we have checked out
all these books for ourselves."
"Lucky us," said Lisa.

“It was nice of Mrs. Page
to loan us the bookmobile,”
said Lisa.
“It was all her idea,”
said Amelia Bedelia.
“Stay here, Sam,” said Lisa.
“And stay away from the books.”

“I found the book,” said Amelia Bedelia.

“Good work,” said Lisa.

“Guess what I found? A thesaurus.”

“Where is it?” asked Amelia Bedelia.

“Right behind you,” said Lisa.

“Run! Hide!” said Amelia Bedelia.

Lisa laughed out loud.

“Come back,” she said.

“A thesaurus is not

a dinosaur, after all.”

“Jeepers,” said Amelia Bedelia.

“Look at all these words.

I can find just the right one to use.”

A man walked up to them.

"I am the manager of this store.

What is all the ruckus about?"

"Ruckus?" said Amelia Bedelia.

"I like that word. Let's look it up.

I would love to use it in a story."

"Ah-hah," said the manager.

"Follow me. You are late."

"I am?" said Amelia Bedelia.

He led them straight to the
children's section of the bookstore.
He said, "I like your costume.
I have never met a storyteller
who dresses like a housekeeper."
Lisa laughed.
Amelia Bedelia did not laugh.
She did not want to disappoint
the manager or the children.

Amelia Bedelia told a terrific story
about dinosaurs attacking the library.
Mrs. Page, the brave librarian,
saved every book from being chomped.
"All in all, it was quite a ruckus,"
said Amelia Bedelia.

"You are great,"
said the children.
"You are talented,"
said the manager.
"You are in trouble,"
said a police officer.

“What’s wrong?” said the manager.

“There must be some mistake.”

“There sure is,” said the officer.

“This lady took that bookmobile.”

“I sure did,” said Amelia Bedelia.

“Mrs. Page told me to.”

"Don't worry,"
said the officer.
"They won't throw
the book at you."
"I hope not,"
said Amelia Bedelia.
"I just bought it."
The officer smiled.
"I will trust you to drive
back to the library,"
she said.

They returned the bookmobile.
"I wonder if Mrs. Page is upset,"
said Amelia Bedelia.
"Why would she be upset?"
said Lisa. "We bought the book."

Mrs. Page was not smiling.
Neither was the woman
standing beside her.

"I owe you an apology,"
said Amelia Bedelia.
"Sam had ruined a book.
You said, 'Go buy the book.'
So we borrowed the bookmobile
and bought the book."

"Oh, dear," said Mrs. Page.

"What happened to our book?

Were the pages torn or just dog-eared?"

"Ask Sam," said Amelia Bedelia.

"He's still digesting it."

“Hey, there! Welcome back,”
said Lisa’s mom.

"I know some other creatures
who would like to say hello."

ARRRRGH!

"I am the word-eating Thesaurus!
If you need a better word,
look inside me!"

"I am the Flying Periodical.
I buzz by every week!"

"I am the Giant Prehistoric Bookworm!

If I had a nose, it would be in a book."

The woman who had not smiled
was now laughing.
"You are all amazing," she said.

"I have been the head librarian
for twenty years,
but I have never seen children
have such fun with books."

“Lisa’s mom helped everyone,”
said Amelia Bedelia.
“So you are the head librarian.
I have heard all about you.
You are the know-it-all
who has been around forever.”

Mrs. Page was about to faint.
The woman laughed and said,
"I guess I am a dinosaur."
"Let's check," said Amelia Bedelia.
"Is your last name Saurus?"
"No," she said, "it is Cramer."
"I am sorry," said Amelia Bedelia.
"You cannot be a dinosaur."
"What a relief," said Mrs. Cramer.

"There is a big parade next week,"
Mrs. Cramer said.
"Would you all march for the library?"

YIPPEE! HOORAY!

On the day of the parade
Amelia Bedelia stopped by the library.
"Amelia Bedelia," said Mrs. Page,
"I *am* glad to see you.
Come see what Mark made for you."

Amelia Bedelia looked up
at the ceiling.
"Is that a mobile?" she asked.

"It is a *book* mobile," said Mrs. Page.

"How sweet," said Amelia Bedelia.

"Just remember," said Mrs. Page.
"You can borrow the books
but not the bookmobile."
They laughed.
Then they went out together
to watch the parade.

READ A BOOK